THE
TOAD THAT
TAUGHT FLYING

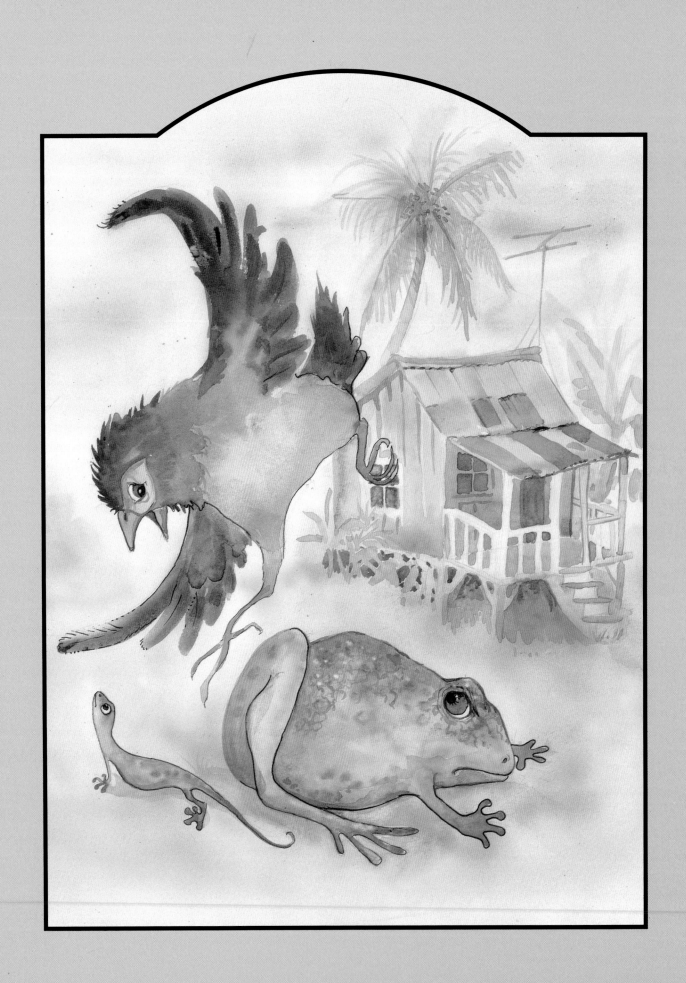

THE TOAD THAT TAUGHT FLYING

story by
MALIA MANESS

illustrations by
PAT HALL

Pacific Greetings

Kamuela, Hawaii

Library of Congress Catalog Card Number. 93-86144

ISBN 0-9633493-1-7

First Printing, 1993

Available from:
Pacific Greetings • P.O. Box 428 • Kamuela, HI 96743
(808) 885-4439 • FAX (808) 885-8203

~Pacific Greetings~

Printed in Hong Kong

DEDICATED

to

our mother and grandmother

LEVERNE

our special

THANK YOU

to

RUTH TABRAH

for her help, encouragement, and editing

Kama clutched the edge of the tin roof below his nest. Today was a scary day. His parents had told him he must begin to fly.

"Don't worry. Just try it!" chirped a gecko who was watching him. "Every baby mynah bird I've ever known has learned to fly.

"But what if I can't!" said Kama.

He didn't want to look down at the ground below because it made his knees weak.

"Flap your wings to get them warmed up and then just jump. That's how they do it! Trust me!" said the gecko.

Kama gave his wings a few flaps. He closed his eyes. He teetered on the edge of the tin roof and ...

JUMPPED!

CRASH!

Kama fell through a ginger plant
and landed on the ground with a

THUD!

Two sparrows were looking
down at him from the ginger plant
and twittering with laughter.
"What a silly baby!" one sparrow
said to the other.

Kama picked himself up and flapped a few steps to get a drink from a nearby puddle.

On the far side of the puddle was a toad.

"Well I wouldn't call you silly," said the toad, "but I've never seen a mynah as clumsy as you seem to be! However," admitted the toad "I'm not very graceful myself."

"I don't want to be clumsy." said Kama. "I just want to fly, and I don't know how."

"I'm sorry little bird," said the toad, "but I can't help you with flying. I can only hop!"

"Maybe I could learn to hop!" said Kama. "Could you teach me how?"

"Sure, it's really quite simple," said the toad. "Just bend your legs at the knee and then straighten them fast so that you shoot into the air like this."

Toad bent his legs, straightened them fast, shot up into the air, and landed a few feet away.

"Wow!" said Kama, "That's almost like flying!"

"That looked easy! I'll give it a try. Here I go!" said Kama.

He bent his knees, straightened his legs, but instead of shooting into the air he tripped and landed face down in the grass.

"I never saw such a clumsy bird!" said the gecko.

"That's not being clumsy. That's trying to learn," said the toad. "Just try it again, Kama. Practice makes perfect!"

Kama got up to try again. This time he shot into the air and landed next to the toad.

"Wow! That was fun!" said Kama.

"A much better hop!" said the toad.

"Not bad." said the gecko.

"Now try again, and this time flap your wings a little," the toad suggested.

Kama tried a third time. This time
he flapped his wings while he hopped.
"Wow! I can! I'm hopping higher,
and higher, and higher!" Kama yelled.

He hopped and flapped around the old house that had his nest on the roof. The more he hopped and the harder he flapped the higher he went.

Kama's mother and father, who were watching him from a nearby palm tree, were astonished.

"Kama has his own way of learning how to fly," said his mother.

"He's a slow learner, but he got there!" Kama's father squawked. He flew off to wait for Kama on the rooftop. Kama's mother flew there too.

"I can hop! I can hop!"

"NO! I CAN FLY!!" squawked Kama. It was a squawk of pure joy.

He flew up, up, and up until he could see his parents on the tin roof. He saw the palm tree, the pig with her piglets, the lady who lived in the house following her dog home, a truck and, so small that Kama almost couldn't see him, ...Toad.

Kama flew down again. It wasn't a very graceful landing, but he landed right next to Toad.

"What a flying instructor! Wow!" said Kama, embracing his friend.

"Flying instructor?" grumbled the gecko, "every baby mynah bird I've ever known has always learned to fly. Toad a teacher? Bah! "

"Toad is the very best of teachers!" said Kama. "He not only taught me how to fly, he taught me to believe that I could. He taught me that falling, flopping, and hopping may be clumsy, but its just part of <u>learning</u>. Thank you, Toad!"